PUFFIN BOOKS
Editor: Kaye Webb

Puss and Cat

Cat and Puss were twins. Their mother had started off with the very best intentions, giving them two sensible names that couldn't be made into something silly just because they were twins, but their big brother Tom couldn't (or wouldn't) say their proper names, which were Katherine and Priscilla, so Cat and Puss they became. They grew up just alike. They weighed the same, their hair was the same, they even had the same wobbly teeth and the same number of chicken-pox spots as each other, and of course they had great fun muddling all the teachers and generally playing tricks on everybody.

But when they were nine, things changed. Tom started it by telling them they were like one person split in two, both halves doing and thinking exactly the same. 'I expect each of you've only got about half the ordinary-sized brain,' he said, and the girls found this so infuriating that they immediately decided to do everything differently. It was only after they had gone out separately to buy birthday presents for their mother and chosen the same thing, and decided separately to go swimming and bumped into each other in the water, that they realized they would have to think very hard indeed and be very brave if they were really going to be separate people.

Catherine Storr is the author of *Clever Polly and the Stupid Wolf* and *Polly and the Wolf Again* (both in Young Puffins), and of *Marianne Dreams*, for older readers.

Catherine Storr

Puss and Cat

Illustrated by Carolyn Dinan

Puffin Books
in association with Faber & Faber

Puffin Books, Penguin Books Ltd,
Harmondsworth, Middlesex, England
Penguin Books, 625 Madison Avenue,
New York, New York 10022, U.S.A.
Penguin Books Australia Ltd,
Ringwood, Victoria, Australia
Penguin Books Canada Ltd, 2801 John Street,
Markham, Ontario, Canada L3R 1B4
Penguin Books (N.Z.) Ltd, 182–190 Wairau Road,
Auckland 10, New Zealand

First published by Faber & Faber 1969
Published in Puffin Books 1978

Made and printed in Great Britain by
Hazell Watson & Viney Ltd,
Aylesbury, Bucks
Set in Linotype Pilgrim

I

Cat and Puss were twins.

When they were born, and had taken everyone by surprise by being two babies instead of the one that had been expected, their mother had said to their father, '... and let's give them *sensible* names. Don't let's call them anything embarrassing or silly.'

'Of course we won't. What sort of silliness?'

'I had a great-aunt who called her twins Adam and Eve. But of course one of them was a boy.'

'Better than Cain and Abel. If they'd both been boys, she could have. You mean we shouldn't call them Lily and Rose? Because I hadn't really considered it.'

'No, I meant names that people could make into silly nicknames. Like Henny and Penny, for Henrietta and Penelope, or Lottie and Tottie, or anything like that.'

'You'll never find names that no one can turn into something silly,' the twins' father had said.

But the twins' mother had believed that she could. She thought about it for a long time, and at last she decided on Katherine and Priscilla. 'Because I like even the little names, if they must get shortened. Kate, and Katie, and Cilla. They're all pretty,' she said.

'Suppose it's Prissy? Do you like that?'

'Not much. But I'm going to make sure they get called by their proper names from the beginning. I'm sure if we start them off right, people are much less likely to think up ridiculous names for them later,' their mother said.

But she hadn't reckoned with her son, Tom. Tom was three. He now found himself elder brother to a couple of

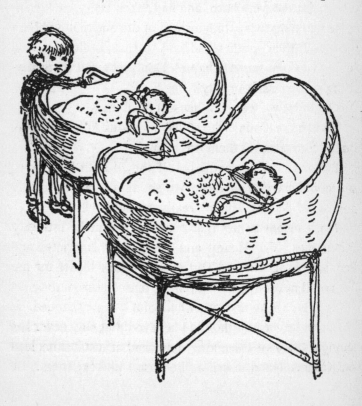

small, unpleasing objects, who took up a great deal of his parents' time and attention, and to him it all seemed hardly worth while. He took as little notice of them as he could, and became suddenly extremely naughty. So when his mother told him that the names of his new sisters were Katherine and Priscilla, he refused even to try to pronounce them, and called the twins distantly and disapprovingly, 'those'. This was bad enough. But a week or so later, when his mother heard him calling the twins by name, she was horrified.

'*What* did you call her, Tom? What did you say?'

'Said, Puss.'

'No! No, Tom, no. She's not called Puss. She's Priscilla.'

'Puss.'

'Say Priscilla.'

'Puss.'

'Tom. Say Priscilla. Be a clever boy. Say Priscilla.'

'Puss.'

His mother changed the subject.

'Look at Katherine, Tom. Say Katherine.'

Tom took one look at Katherine and said distinctly, 'Cat.'

'Tom, love. I know you can say it beautifully for me. Say Kath-er-ine.'

Tom said 'Cat'. He was intelligent and determined. He was also the only person in the household who never had any difficulty in telling the babies apart. 'I can't think how he knows, because he doesn't ever look at them,' his mother said. 'And if I say "which is Priscilla?" or "which is Katherine?" he doesn't answer. He'll only tell me if I use the names he does.'

That was how the twins became Puss and Cat.

2

People think about you differently if you are twins.

It was lucky for Puss and Cat that they couldn't remember all the occasions when they were babies when their mother was stopped by dear old ladies, who leaned over the double pram, and crooned, 'Aren't they sweet? Exactly alike, aren't they? Two boys or two girls? What are they called?' Later, when they were walking, they were given more biscuits, apples and sweets by kind and interested shopkeepers, the traffic was held up especially for them more often, they were more talked to by total strangers, more whispered about, more stared at than any ordinary single child. Their mother was irritated and amused. 'You'd think they were some sort of circus. You'd think no one had ever seen twins before. If they were monsters I don't believe it could be any worse,' she said.

'Perhaps it'll get better as they grow up a bit. They can't go *on* looking exactly alike,' her husband said.

He was wrong. They did.

Their mother did the best she could. She dressed them in different colours. 'But that only helps when you see them together. When they're apart you still don't know which is which,' people complained.

'Puss shall wear red and Cat blue. Each of them can have a colour and stick to it,' she said. But that didn't work either. The twins wouldn't stick to their own colours. They wore each other's clothes, and the muddle was worse than ever.

'Now their hair is beginning to grow, it will be easier. Puss shall have her hair cut short and Cat shall have pigtails,' their mother said.

This might have been the answer, if the twins hadn't had such thick hair. Combing out Puss's short hair was bad enough, but Cat went through agonies every night and every morning. Her piercing shrieks could be heard all over the house. Her mother persisted for several months, and Cat's hair was just below her shoulders, when one evening it all got too much for everyone. Cat's hair had been particularly tangled by the wind, she'd fought against the combing and brushing even more loudly than usual, and in the middle of it all Puss picked up her mother's nail scissors and, before anyone could stop her, cut off a handful of Cat's hair quite short, shorter than her own. There was nothing for it but to take her to the hairdresser the next day, and have the rest of her hair trimmed to the same length. And quite soon Cat's hair had grown a little, and Puss's had to be cut, and there wasn't any difference between them again.

They went on looking alike in every other way too.

When Puss grew two inches in a year, so did Cat. When Cat weighed four and a half stone, so did Puss. When Puss was six, she fell off her bicycle and knocked out one of her front teeth. They were her first, baby teeth, and a week later Cat's front tooth just dropped out naturally. (It came out in a ham sandwich, as a matter of fact, but that counts as natural.) And it was the same front tooth, the left top one, that Puss had lost, of course. Cat and Puss even had little jagged scars almost in the same place on their left thumbs, just below the joint. Cat's had been made by a tin-opener and Puss had done hers with a chisel, but you couldn't have told the difference once they'd healed. It was extraordinary how exactly alike they were. Their mother was in despair.

'Perhaps when they go to school they'll want to be different,' she thought.

But Puss and Cat didn't want to be different at school. It was too amusing to be just the same. They changed desks, they changed names, they changed clothes. They could muddle everyone. If one of them had talked when she should have been silent, done her sums wrong, forgotten to feed the goldfish, come in late, or brought the wrong books to class, no one knew which twin deserved to be scolded. If one was asked to a party, picked for a team, chosen to sing in the school choir, act in the school play, go on a school outing, both turned up, and each said, 'But you told *me* to come.' Some of the children knew which was Puss and which was Cat, but none of the teachers did. They got used to treating them always together, it was easier that way. If they'd both been there when the orders were given, neither of them could say afterwards that she hadn't heard. If both of them were punished for what one of them had done, it was fair enough, since neither would say that she had or hadn't done it. And it was easier, too, to call each of them PussCat, without trying to discover which really was which. They didn't mind.

They were in the same class, of course. They got about the same marks. If, one term, Puss did better at music and reading, while Cat was better at sums and art, the next term it would be the other way round. They learned to swim in the same week, they played rounders and netball equally well. They had measles starting on the same day, and when they had chicken pox, they had the same number of spots. They said they had counted. They were exactly the same. There had never been twins more exactly alike.

3

Then, when the twins were nine, things became different.

It started with their mother's birthday present. Her birthday, not theirs. They had always given her a present from both of them. One year it had been a bath-sponge. Another year it was a ballpoint pen, with twelve different colours inside its body. Last year they had given her a salt and pepper to match. 'The salt's from Cat, and the pepper's from Puss,' they had said. This year their mother had mentioned that she wanted little handkerchiefs, all different colours, a rainbow present. Or she'd like some pastry cutters, different shapes. She would like to make biscuits like hearts, like spades, like diamonds and clubs. Or she'd always thought it would be nice to have grey note-paper, with envelopes to match. There were a lot of things she'd like to have as presents, but didn't feel like buying for herself. 'That's the best sort of present. A luxury you know you oughtn't to afford,' she said.

Puss and Cat said nothing.

Later, in the room they shared at the top of the house,

Puss said, 'What are you going to give Mum for her birthday?' Always, before, she or Cat would have said, 'What are *we* going to give Mum?'

Cat said, 'I don't know. What are you?'

'I don't want to get her hankies. Or those biscuit-cutting things.'

'I think paper and envelopes are boring. Let's think of something else.'

This was two weeks before the day. When the twins were out shopping the next Saturday morning, they walked round Woolworth's four or five times, eyeing everything. Talcum powder? Stockings? Pencils? A blue glass vase? They came out silently, empty-handed. There was still another Saturday to find something in, there was plenty of time.

At breakfast on that next Saturday, Cat said, 'I'm going shopping early.'

'Could you go to the grocer's and see if their special cooking oil has come in? I ordered one of those big tins, but it wouldn't be too heavy if you and Puss took my shopping trolley and pulled it up the hill between you,' her mother said.

'I'm going by myself,' } Cat and Puss said, at the
'I'm not going with her,' } same moment.

'I'll pick it up in the car this afternoon,' their father said.

Directly after breakfast Puss disappeared. Later in the morning Cat went out alone. They came in to lunch separately, both hugging themselves, their eyes bright with secrets.

'You look pleased with yourselves,' Tom said.

'Not specially,' Puss said, just as Cat said, 'We are, rather.'

'Make up your minds!'

'We don't have to be the same. She might be pleased, and me not.'

'You have to be both the same,' Tom said.

'Why?'

'Because you're twins. Didn't you know?'

'Know what?'

'You have to do everything the same when you're twins. You can't really choose, any more than you chose to be born on the same day. Whatever you think you've chosen, either of you, it'll always turn out to be exactly what the other one chose. You can't help it, you're just made that way.'

'Tom, you're talking nonsense,' his mother said.

'I'm not. It's been proved, scientifically, twins are always like that. Look how Puss and Cat both don't like macaroni cheese and do like spaghetti. And how when we play the word game they always think of the same word. And when they play cards they're always either both lucky or both unlucky. They even have nightmares on the same night. It's like being one person split in two halves. One half is Puss, and the other half is Cat.'

'We aren't. I'm a whole person, and so is Cat.'

'It's not true. I'm separate from Puss, and she's separate from me.'

'We don't always do everything the same.'

'We often do things separately, quite different.'

'Lots of people don't like macaroni cheese. It's too squiggly.'

'Heaps of people have nightmares.'

'We think different things.'

'We say different things.'

'Like now? You're both of you saying exactly the same,' Tom said.

'We weren't.'

'You were. I expect each of you've only got about half the ordinary-sized brain. Sometimes you sound like that.'

'Tom, don't tease,' his mother said.

'We don't care. We're as clever as he is,' Puss said.

'You might be, put together. Separately you're only half as clever, perhaps not as much as that.'

'You're jealous because you aren't twins,' Cat said.

'Why should I want to be twins? I'd rather be a whole person by myself. I'd rather be me,' Tom said.

'We'd rather be us.'

But was it true? After lunch, Puss said to Cat, 'Do we always do everything the same?'

'If we do, let's not.'

'I bought Mum's birthday present this morning.'

Cat said, 'So did I.'

'But we didn't buy them together. Let's do everything different. I don't want to be just the same as you. You don't want to be just like me, do you?'

'We've started being different, anyway. Buying Mum's presents separately,' Cat said.

Sunday was their mother's birthday. Her breakfast plate was piled with parcels, there were flowers on the table, her husband cooked the meal, special food. Fried potatoes mixed with little slivers of crisp bacon, baby sausages sunburned brown, creamy eggs. Hot coffee. Grapefruit, a special treat. Puss and Cat didn't like it, it was too bitter.

After breakfast, their mother opened her presents. A dressing-gown, pretty, frilly, with a nightdress to match, from her husband. Lots of kitchen gadgets from Tom – a garlic presser, a rubber spatula, an elaborate instrument which opened tins, took off crown corks and cracked nuts, all in one. A serrated knife for cutting tomatoes. A patent cheese grater of a quite new kind. (They discovered later that it only worked on cheese that was rock hard with age.)

Puss had done her present up in pink tissue paper. Cat's was in turquoise blue. They looked pretty, side by side.

'Which shall I open first?' their mother asked.

'Hers,' Cat said.

'Mine last,' Puss said.

'You each open your own, then. That way I'll see both at the same time.'

Puss untied the silver string and undid the pink paper carefully. Cat pulled the black ribbon off her parcel, and tore the turquoise paper. Each twin unwrapped her own present, and looked across to see what the other had bought.

'You saw what I'd got, and copied! Copy cat!' said Puss.

'I didn't! You guessed from what I said on Friday,' said Cat.

'I got mine first.'

'I'd decided what to buy long before you went out, even.'

'It doesn't matter,' their mother said quickly.

'It does. It's silly. You can't wear two shower caps at once.'

'You could if you had two heads,' Tom said.

'Two heads are better than one.'

'Not on Mummy.'

'I'll wear them on alternate days.'

'But they're exactly the same. You won't know which is which.'

'They're terribly pretty. Thank you so much, Puss – Cat. Just what I wanted.'

'But you didn't want two. No one could want two.'

'Don't cry, Puss. Don't cry, Cat.'

'I thought I'd found just exactly the right thing. All by myself,' Cat said.

'That's what I thought too,' Puss said.

'Well, you did. It is exactly what I wanted. You both had the same good idea.'

Tom looked across the table at the twins. He didn't mean to be unkind, but he couldn't help saying in his look, 'I told you so. You can't be different, even if you try.'

4

'We must be different,' Puss and Cat said to each other. They said it almost every day. But how? It wasn't easy.

'Let's go to school separately. You go down past the shops, and I'll go by the lane,' Cat said.

'That won't make us different.'

'It'd be a start.'

'Couldn't we be different at school?'

'How?'

'You be good, and me be naughty.'

'Or me naughty, and you good. We could take it in turns.'

So on Wednesday, Cat was good and Puss was bad. She talked all through singing, and got sent out of the class. She wrote 'I love the BEATLES' on the classroom blackboard in five different-coloured chalks just before the Natural History lesson. She played noughts and crosses with herself all over her sum book instead of doing long multiplication, and in the afternoon she went into the cloakroom and mixed up the other children's shoes and coats so that there was pandemonium when the time came for them to go home. There was an almighty fuss, and Puss was to be punished the next day.

But the next day, Thursday, it was Cat's turn. Cat filled the empty ink-wells with Epsom Salts, brought from home, so that when Miss Bolton filled them up, they foamed, and inky, blue bubbles ran down over the desks. Cat spent the art lesson modelling snakes of different sizes, a whole family of serpents, with black charcoal eyes, instead of the coil pot she'd been told to make. At lunch she constructed a desert landscape of shepherd's pie, with green oases made of cabbage in a wilderness of mince and potato, peopled with fragments of dark crust of bread. After lunch, she played Chopsticks loudly on the piano in the hall, and then led an expedition over the school wall to the building site next door, where the workmen gave them a handful of shiny new nails apiece to take back as trophies.

On Friday the twins were told to report to Miss Stephens's room to be talked to.

'Katherine and Priscilla, do you realize how troublesome you've been these last two days? I've never known you behave so badly before. Interrupting the lessons! Making confusion in the cloakrooms! Annoying the teachers! Trespassing on the building site!'

'We didn't do the same things.'

'I wrote "The Beatles" on the blackboard,' said Puss.

'I put the salts into the ink-wells,' said Cat.

'I talked in singing.'

'I made the snakes in Art.'

'It doesn't matter who did which. You were both disobedient and impertinent. You must both be punished. And don't let it happen again.'

Puss and Cat had to apologize to the teachers, and do extra sums indoors, while the rest of the class was outside in the playground during the mid-morning and lunch breaks that day and the next. It didn't make them feel any better to find that they both had to say they were sorry for each wickedness that either of them had done. They weren't good at sums. Puss got three out of twelve right, and so did Cat. They scowled at each other across the desks. It was maddening to be alike in this too.

'We might try again this weekend,' Cat said, that Friday evening.

'Tomorrow we'll go out separately. I won't tell you where I'm going, and you shan't tell me,' Puss said.

'Go out? What for?'

'I don't know yet. But for different things. Then everyone will see that we're separate.'

Cat spent Saturday morning thinking what she could do that Puss wouldn't think of. Go for a bicycle ride? It was something they had often done together. Go to the pond on the common to look for tadpoles? It was too early in the year. Stay at home and read? Go down to the library for some new books? Ask Mum if she could cook something new? Tidy out her cupboard? Everything seemed boring, and she was sure Puss would have thought of doing something much more exciting.

But at lunch she decided. She would bicycle down to the baths and swim. She would practise her underwater swimming. Neither she nor Puss could stay down for a whole width of the baths. Perhaps she'd get good enough to swim a length along the bottom of the bath. Puss wouldn't be able to, and then they'd really be different.

'Can I go swimming?' she asked her mother.

'Isn't it too cold?'

'The water's always warm. I needn't stay in very long.'

'Not more than half an hour, then. How much does it cost? I never can remember.'

'Ten pence.'

'Take 5op out of my purse. You and Puss can buy something to eat on the way back with what's left over.'

'We're not both going,' Cat said quickly.

'Is Puss ill?'

'No. We don't always have to go everywhere together.'

'Take twenty-five pence, then. And be careful how you cycle.'

Cat rode off alone, pleased that she'd thought of this and was doing it by herself. And the swimming baths were lovely, not too full, plenty of room for practising. Cat swam up and down the length, breast stroke, side stroke and butterfly; she wasn't very good at this last one. She dived in from the side and from the lowest board. She threw one of the rope quoits to the bottom and dived for it. She hadn't learned to keep her eyes open under water. The first time she found the quoit by luck, she'd dived exactly on top of it. But after that she kept on missing it, she couldn't find it by groping. She had to open her eyes for a moment. She saw the ring, lying quivering and enormous on the white tiled floor of the bath, and grasped it. She became braver. After she'd successfully blinked her eyes open two or three times, she kept them open for longer. It was easier, too, when she could see where she was, to stay down.

She swam half a width, then the whole way. It wasn't as difficult as she'd expected. After a short time she decided to see how much of a length she could manage. She dived down at the shallow end and swam as far as she could towards the diving boards at the deep end, holding an enormous breath, her eyes wide open all the time.

Someone else was swimming towards her. The some-

one else was under the water too. The someone else was also wearing a white cap and the black regulation swimsuit. The someone else wasn't very large. About Cat's own size. They came face to face, and both of them rose, gasping, to the surface. The other person was, of course, Puss.

They rode their bicycles back together. There didn't seem any point in not. But they hardly spoke. There wasn't anything agreeable to say.

5

'It's desperate. *Why* do we always think the same? It's awful being twins,' Puss said to herself.

'I'm fed up. Why does Puss always choose whatever I'm doing? Can't we ever be separate people?' Cat asked inside her head.

Cat and Puss were annoyed with each other. They had often quarrelled in the past, but now it seemed they could hardly speak to each other politely. Whatever one said, the other contradicted. Alone in their room at night, they often hardly exchanged a word.

Puss lay in her bed and thought. She had to do something which would show everyone how completely different she was from Cat.

'Suppose I did something tremendous? Saved someone from burning to death in a fire? Caught a bank robber? Acted on television? Then people would know I was Puss. No. They'd know I was Priscilla. Cat wouldn't count,' she thought. Cat, pretending to be asleep in her bed, was wondering, 'There must be some way of proving we're two separate people. Suppose I looked quite different somehow? Or if I did something splendid, like saving a drowning man? Or wrote a poem that got printed in a newspaper? Or was chosen to jump a horse in the Olympic games? People wouldn't muddle us up if I did something like that.'

'Perhaps I ought to do something terrible. Cat'd never be really wicked. I could steal out of a shop – travel without a ticket – cheat in exams. If I was sent to prison, and Cat was free, then everyone would be able to tell which of us was which,' Puss thought.

'Suppose I died? Then there'd only be one of us, and no one would expect Puss to be different from ordinary people. Or if she died, I'd be ordinary. But I don't want Puss to die. I don't want to be dead. I want to be ordinary and alive. I want to be me, by myself, just one of me. Me,' thought Cat.

At almost the same moment, which would have annoyed them very much if they'd known it, the twins fell asleep.

It was hot. It was summer. The pavements smelled of hot dust, people sat at little tables outside coffee shops, drinking cold drinks and eating ices with little tinny spoons. The chestnut tree strewed pink blossoms in the road: inside each little flower were long white stamens, and there were orange spots on the pale flower tissue. A blackbird sat every evening on the top of the aspen poplar and sang arpeggios to the dark blue air. Cat and Puss went to bed in the daylight, saw the young moon gradually come alight as she sank into the darkening western sky, heard voices and footsteps in the road outside as they lay in bed. Other people were just starting to wake up and live for the long light evenings, as they fell asleep. When they woke in the mornings, the sun was high, birds had already fallen silent after their first excited clamour at dawn. Days lasted for ever. Voices echoed in the swimming baths, warm air circled round under thin cotton frocks, you could move anywhere, do anything, without the fear of being cold. Even the rain fell warm, like a blessing. The summer raced by. Strawberries, raspberries, two days that were so hot and damp it felt like living in warm cotton wool; then a night of thunderstorms, lashing rain, big hailstones rattling on the garage roof, the next day the smell of wet grass, all the trees dripping. It was almost a relief to be cool again. It was nearly the end of the school term.

'I want to go on holiday by myself,' Puss said to her mother.

'Where? How?'

'Joanna's going to a children's holiday camp. You learn how to put up a tent and track through a forest. They do first aid and things. And cook over a camp fire. It'd be fun. Can I?'

'Can I go pony trekking? Alone? Without Puss?' Cat asked.

'I shall go sailing with the Swallow club. On the Norfolk Broads,' said Tom.

So they were all to go off separately. The children's mother and father thought that perhaps it was a good idea. 'Puss and Cat will be better apart. They want to be as different as possible. This is one way of doing it,' their mother said, and her husband agreed. 'And Tom will be better without any of us for a time. He needs to get away from the family too,' he said.

'It's the first time we haven't all been together for the summer holidays,' Tom's mother said.

'Good for the children to be on their own, and splendid for us. We'll drive around and see the West Country a bit by ourselves.'

Puss and Cat didn't talk to each other much about what they were going to do. Each of them had her secret doubts. 'Sleeping in a tent! I wonder if the ground's very hard and lumpy? There'll be earwigs, I shouldn't wonder. And spiders. And I'll have to learn to light a fire with only one match, Joanna says. And cook,' Puss thought. The only things she knew how to cook were toffee and chocolate crispies. And she hated insects, anything with lots of legs that scuttled, or with furry wings that flapped.

'Riding. I'm terrified,' Cat thought. Cat had never been

a proper horse girl. She liked reading about horses, and in imagination she won gymkhanas, jumped five-barred gates at pony trials, galloped furiously across downland carrying secret messages to beleaguered troops. When she actually met a horse, she was scared silly. She was frightened of the horse's head end in case it bit her, of its other end in case it kicked. When she was in the saddle she was frightened of falling off. She had learned to ride because, although she was frightened of all these things, she was even more frightened of being frightened. And she wasn't very good. On a pony trekking week there would be girls much better than she was, brave girls with lean clever bodies and well arranged long straight hair who would leap their ponies over hedges and ditches, gallop fearlessly along sandy beaches, groom the animals confidently and expertly, and talk to each other knowingly about all sorts of things Cat didn't understand. She knew she wasn't going to be much good at any of it, but she had to try. She had to do something Puss couldn't.

It was easier for Tom. He just wanted to sail. He didn't have to try hard to be anything different, he was just himself.

6

Term ended. The holidays came, there was a round of visits to be made to school outfitters, and other shops, to dentists, to grandparents and distant cousins and aunts. Then the smell of stations, of railway coaches, of hot tarmac roads, new country smells at unknown destinations. Tom, Priscilla and Katherine were at their different holiday camps. They weren't very far apart, but they didn't meet, they were all too busy doing their different things. Tom was on the Broads, Priscilla camping in a wood in the same county, but right inland. Katherine was on a farm not very near either of the others, but still just within the reach of both of them. 'It'll be comforting for you to know you can see each other if you really want,' the children's mother had said. Priscilla and Katherine had said immediately, and together, 'We shan't.'

The children's parents drove off together to the West of England, where they had friends. They were going to stay in several different houses in Devon and Cornwall, were going to visit places they had never seen, might fly out for a day or two to the Scilly Isles. Picture postcards arrived nearly every day at the sailing club, at the camp, at the farm. Wild ponies on moors, great cliffs towering above calm silver beaches, King Arthur's Castle, Merlin's cave, a lighthouse, stormy waves, a deserted pool, showed Tom and Priscilla and Katherine the sort of country their mother and father were visiting. In return they wrote brief, hurried cards. 'Primrose jumped a wall two feet high and I didn't fall off.' 'I took the sailing canoe out yesterday and got nearly a mile upstream.' 'Tomorrow night we are going on a midnight trek. We might see a fox.' 'This morning we capsized, it is raining, and I am rather wet.' 'I have learned how to put on a double bridle. We rode fifteen miles yesterday, I am sore underneath.' 'I was cook on Sunday, I made an omelette with things in it, it was fine.'

Tom sailed. He learned how to make fast the sheet, when to tack, how to use the wind to send him in whatever direction he wanted to go. He lived on a moored houseboat with twenty other boys. They were never quite dry, and not always warm. They were always hungry, and they ate whatever the older ones among them could cook. Tins and tins of soup, spaghetti and baked beans. Pounds of apples and cheese. Tom thought about sailing, dreamed about sailing, lived sailing. He had not time to wonder what the rest of the family was doing. He was almost perfectly happy.

Priscilla lived in a tent. She slept in a sleeping-bag on a ground sheet. She learned how to pitch a tent and how to strike it; she learned how to build a camp fire out of kindling and twigs, how to balance a saucepan on the fire to cook, how to toast bacon on sharpened slivers of wood in the flames, and how to bake potatoes in the hot ashes. She learned how to leave a trail that couldn't be covered up or disturbed by accident, and how to follow someone else's track. She learned how to read a map and use a compass, how to guess by her shadow what was the time of day, how to tie knots, recognize a distress signal, give first aid. She learned to shut farmers' gates, to avoid trampling over crops, to move silently at night; she learned the names of trees and how to tell which was which by the bark and the leaves and the shape of their growing. She began to learn which mushrooms and toadstools you could eat, and which you couldn't. It was fun and it was exciting, and Priscilla loved it.

Katherine was the only one of the three who slept in a proper bed. She stayed on a farm, which was also a riding school. Every morning she and the others got up at seven o'clock and cleaned out the stables, groomed the ponies and fed them. The ponies had oats, the riders ate porridge, there wasn't much difference between them, Katherine thought. After breakfast they exercised the ponies in the lanes round the farm, or practised for gymkhanas in the field where low jumps were set up. In the afternoons they went out on treks, along roads, through fields and woods and over the heath. Katherine found everything they did frightening. In the morning the ponies were fresh and difficult to control. Primrose had a way of dancing backwards and bucking when she was asked to do anything she hadn't decided to do by herself. Stubbs, the fat grey, did everything in slow motion for three quarters of an hour, and then suddenly responded to the kicks and proddings of his rider by flying off at a vehement canter that was almost a gallop, and stopped equally suddenly after a few hundred yards. Katherine generally fell off when this happened. She was terrified of the jumps. 'You must NOT hold on to the saddle, Katherine,' the beautiful, scornful, frightening instructress, whose name was Diana, said to her sternly.

'But if I don't I fall off.'

'No you won't. Grip with your knees. Now try again.'

Katherine tried, but Primrose stopped short of the jump.

'She doesn't want to.'

'Never mind if she wants to or not, you've got to make her go over.'

The next time Primrose cantered up to the jump, swerved sideways and bucked.

'You pulled her back.'

'I didn't mean to.'

'Try again. She mustn't get away with anything, it'll ruin her character.'

Katherine thought that her own character was probably being ruined while Primrose's was being improved.

'Now make her canter! Take her right up to it! Keep

your weight forward, help her over!' Diana shouted. Primrose sidled and danced and desperately Katherine kicked her sides. Primrose snorted, and quickened her pace. Katherine's hand reached for the saddle. She made a great resolution and didn't allow herself to clutch. Primrose jumped, and Katherine fell off.

'What did you fall off for?' Diana asked crossly.

'I wasn't holding the saddle.'

'I told you, grip with your knees, and keep your balance. Like this.'

Diana put Clarry, her chestnut pony, across three jumps very quickly, and came back to where Katherine was still sitting, rubbing her bruises.

'You just go with the pony. There's no need to fall off. Go on. Get up again quickly, or she'll think she's beaten you.'

Katherine had no doubts but that Primrose knew which of them had been beaten. But she got back into the saddle again, and the lesson went on. She fell off twice more, but the last time, by luck, not skill, found herself still on Primrose's back after the jump as well as before. She was so stiff from the jumping and the afternoon treks that she hurt all over almost all the time. Her bottom was sore and she had a swelling over one eye where her hard hat had bruised her in one of the falls. If she hadn't been dead tired every night her aching muscles would have kept her awake. As it was she dreamed the whole night through of fearful jumps and excited ponies, of overhanging boughs

40

and unexpected pitfalls. But she was called Katherine, she was doing something Puss had never done, and no one even knew that she was a twin. She was terrified, but she went on. She meant to learn to be brave.

7

The sailing, the camping and the riding were to last for two weeks. After that the family would stay, all together again, for another week with the children's grandmother in the country. Then home.

'I shall have sailed a Kestrel by myself. Next year I'll be a mate,' thought Tom.

'I shall pitch a tent in the garden at home. I shall have Ann Marie to stay, and I shall take her tracking and cook her breakfast on a camp fire. I shall tell her that I'm called Priscilla now. If anyone calls me Puss, I shan't answer,' Priscilla thought.

'Tomorrow Diana will say I'm to ride Toby. Toby's nervous. When he's startled he bucks and tries to run away. I saw Toby jump the five-barred gate when the gun went off in the next field. Or it would be worse if I had to take Lady Evelyn out, she's enormous and valuable and gets excited very easily. I've got a pain, I feel sick. I wish I'd never come,' Katherine thought.

It was near the end of the fortnight. Two more nights, a day and a half, and they would see each other again.

Although they weren't more than twenty miles apart, any of them, they felt as if they were in different countries, they felt that months had passed since they had met. They felt they had become different people, different from each other, different from what they had been before. Tom simply knew he was Tom, more Tom than ever. Priscilla and Katherine felt un-twinned, separate. Priscilla and Katherine, Katherine and Priscilla; not a sign of PussCat, different people, with different sorts of lives. It was Priscilla who knew that she felt this and thought about it most. Katherine hadn't time to think about anything but that she must not let anyone guess how frightened she was. She had got to finish her two weeks' riding in style.

That night, the last but one, was horrible. Summer might have come completely to an end, it was so cold. A north-east wind got up towards late evening, getting stronger all the time. 'Winds will approach gale force on the east coast of England' the radio announcer had said on the late news, and the children's parents, three-quarters of the way back from the West Country, looked at each other and said, 'Those poor children!'

'I hope they don't let Tom sail tomorrow,' Tom's mother said.

'Puss will have her tent round her ears. Do you remember the night we camped out in Wales, when the wind blew all the canvas into the next field but one?' Puss's father said.

'Anyway, Cat'll be all right. It's nice to know that one

of them is in a solid brick building,' they said to each other.

It was Katherine, in fact, who was awake. She lay and listened to the wind, which tore at the trees round the farm till they shuddered and groaned, and their branches thrashed the dark sky like the limbs of a man in pain. The wind screamed round the corners of the old building, and whistled through chinks in the woodwork, caught doors out of human hands and sent them slamming against their frames with tremors like earthquakes. And behind the slamming and the banging and the clash of tiles dislodged from the roof, and the straining of gates, loose on their hinges, there was a moan and a murmur. It was a low moan that went on all the time, and could be heard when the other sounds ceased for a moment. It was a distant murmur. The moan was sorrowful. The murmur was angry, and was carried over miles of flat marshland, fringed with acres of writhing sedge grasses. It was the sullen, threatening voice of the North Sea.

Katherine took a long time to get to sleep. When she slept she dreamed of trouble.

The next morning the ground round the riding school was littered with tiles, with twigs and leaves. A gate had been torn off its hinges. One of the little old apple trees was down, and the grass of the orchard was scattered with small green fruit. Katherine helped the others to clear away the wreckage, but she wasn't thinking about what she was doing. Instead she wondered where they would be riding this afternoon, which pony she'd be told to take, whether the wind would make the animals skittish, or frighten them so that they bolted. She was ashamed that she couldn't make herself attend to anything else. She felt sure that Georgie and Gina and Sue and Margie weren't worrying about the afternoon's ride. Probably they were looking forward to their last expedition with the ponies, they were probably longing for gallops. They'd be angry and disappointed if it rained and they weren't able to go. They were confident and careless and brave. Katherine wasn't any of these things, she was just anxious.

After lunch they were told. The trekking party was to go in a direction they'd never taken before. It would mean rather a long time spent on the roads. Katherine's heart lifted, you mustn't gallop on the roads. But they were to try to reach the shore; some of them hadn't yet seen the shore, and it was a splendid place for a gallop. Katherine's heart sank. It would be a long afternoon, they were to start off immediately, take biscuits for tea, be back latish for a farewell supper.

Out in the stable yard, Diana decided who was to ride which pony. Katherine couldn't make up her mind whether she'd feel safer with Primrose or Stubbs. To her relief, Sue was given the unreliable Toby. But then Gina was told to saddle Primrose, and Charlotte got Stubbs. Katherine wondered hopefully if perhaps one of the ponies had gone lame and one rider would have to be left behind. This happy idea had just occurred to her when she heard Diana say, 'Katherine, you take Lady Evelyn out this afternoon. You need shaking up.'

'But I've never ridden Lady Evelyn,' Katherine said.

'That's why I'm telling you to take her out now. Hurry up, we don't want to waste the whole afternoon in the yard.'

Katherine went into Lady Evelyn's box to collect her tack. Her hands shook so that the metal jingled aloud. Lady Evelyn was the largest of the ponies, so high she was almost a horse. She was elegant, Katherine had often admired her looks, but she'd never envied her rider. Lady Evelyn was nervous, shied at loud noises and unexpected objects like white washing blowing on a line, or a train passing on a neighbouring railway embankment. She was known to be jumpy on the roads, and Katherine guessed she'd be over-excited, if not wild, by the sea. Katherine's hands were slippery with fear. She took a long time to fasten the girths and to buckle the cheekstrap. And when she at last finished, and Diana had given the word to mount, she found herself much further from the ground than she'd been used to. It seemed a long way to fall.

When she'd recovered from her first panic, she felt a little better. The roads weren't crowded and Lady Evelyn was quiet on the whole. She had a brisk trot which was quite different from the smaller ponies' and Katherine took time to get used to it, but once she'd learned the rhythm she almost enjoyed it. Her greatest trouble was Lady Evelyn's determination to get ahead of the others. Katherine constantly found herself more than a hundred yards in front of the group, being shouted at angrily by Diana. 'Can't you keep with the rest of us, instead of charging ahead like that?'

'She trots so fast. I think it's because her legs are longer than the others',' Katherine said.

'Well, hold her in, can't you? It isn't as if you knew the country round here. Keep behind me, for Pete's sake.'

Katherine tried to keep behind. The route they were following was complicated, with a great many turnings into lanes, and sometimes short cuts across fields, and she would much have preferred to stay at the back of the party and to follow where Diana led. But Lady Evelyn couldn't trot slowly and wouldn't stay behind. The only way to manage her, Katherine found, was to slow her to a walk at intervals, drop behind the others for a space, and then let Lady Evelyn trot and catch them up again. 'She has a *spanking* trot,' Katherine thought. It was an expression she'd read and she was pleased to be able to use it so aptly. It suited Lady Evelyn down to the ground.

It worked all right once or twice. The third time, Lady Evelyn didn't want to be pulled up, and danced sideways into Joanna, who backed into Sue, who was carried by Toby into a ditch. Diana's look at Katherine was more cutting than any words. When Lady Evelyn had quieted down, Katherine walked her as slowly as she could, letting the others get well ahead. They were actually out of sight round a bend in the road before she let the mare know that she could trot again. But Lady Evelyn showed her independence by taking no notice. She pretended to be more interested in the hedge than in joining the rest of the party. She bent her long neck and chopped the grass at the side of the road – something Diana never allowed. When Katherine pulled her head up hard, she turned and began to sidle back in the wrong direction. It was a little time before Katherine could get her round and moving the right way. She did at last consent to trot, as fast and eagerly as if she hadn't been wasting time. Katherine was used to her paces now and she found she liked the knowledge that she could rise and fall in time with Lady Evelyn's brisk movements. She covered the next stretch

49

of road quickly, rounded the corner, saw an empty few hundred yards ahead of her, and went on, pleased with herself for arranging things so well. Lady Evelyn's hooves made an agreeable pattern of sound on the road, she was moving beautifully, and this was the longest trot Katherine had been able to allow herself. She hoped they wouldn't catch the others up too soon.

The road took several turns. It was impossible to see more than fifty yards or so ahead. It was several minutes before Katherine realized that if the others had kept to the road she must have caught them up by this time. She must have missed some side lane which they had taken. She had no idea where they might be.

She pulled up and turned back, this time at a walking-pace. The road looked unfamiliar, going this way, she didn't recognize anything. Now she saw a lane leading off to the left, a gate leading into a field on the right. Further back another little road joined the one she was on. But she couldn't remember if she'd passed that after she'd lost sight of the others, or before. She was bewildered. She was hopelessly lost.

8

Priscilla was bored. The last day of the camping holiday should have been spent in a visit to the coast in a specially chartered coach; but everything had gone wrong. The blizzard of the night before had snapped tent ropes, blown the roof off the storage shed, and scattered refuse all over the three-acre field. A large branch had come down from the big oak tree, and was blocking the lane which led up to the camp site. There was a great deal of clearing away to be done before the camp was fit to leave for the day, and before the coach could get near enough to pick them up. Priscilla hated tidying, even if it was a tent instead of her room, and a field instead of the garden at home. She was feeling short-tempered by the time they were free to climb into the coach, and not pleased to find herself sitting next to Stella, who had camped before, and who knew everything a little better than she did.

'I've had a horrible morning. This is better,' Priscilla said, bouncing on the springy seat at the back of the coach.

'Last year when we went to the sea, it was boiling. We

just sat and baked on the beach, and swam, and then baked again. There wasn't a breath of wind,' Stella said.

'I've brought my swimming things.'

'You won't be able to swim. For one thing, it's too cold, for another the sea'll be terribly rough. There'll be much more wind when we reach the shore even than there is here,' Stella said.

'I could paddle, anyway.'

'Paddling's what babies do.'

'I like paddling,' Priscilla said stoutly.

'Wait till you get there. You've no idea what the North Sea's like till you've been in it.'

They seemed to be in the coach for hours. Priscilla was sleepy, Stella felt sick. When at last they climbed out, they were all drowsy, cold, cramped, their behinds numb with sitting for so long. They were decanted on a long straight road which seemed to come from nowhere and to lead to nowhere. On one side were marshes and dykes : a flat, flat country, across which the wind howled under a sky lumpy with grey, cotton wool clouds. On the other side was a long ridge of sand dunes, grey-green with long sharp marram grass. It was cool and very windy. There was no beach to be seen, and no sky.

'Where—?' Priscilla asked.

'Over there. Behind the dunes.'

Some of them started to climb. When Priscilla hauled herself over the top, she saw a long flat beach stretching away towards a tumbling, angry sea. The next moment the wind had filled her eyes with water and the loose sand flew into her face and hair and stung her ankles between her jeans and her shoes.

'Feel like paddling in that?' Stella asked scornfully.

'I might.'

'You're crazy. I'm getting out of this wind.'

Priscilla wouldn't have minded getting out of it too, but she was proud. Stella slid down the dunes, back towards the road. Priscilla began to fight her way towards the edge of the sea. It was terribly hard going, and she was alone. Everyone else, it seemed, had stayed on the road side of the sand dunes. Priscilla didn't mind, it made her feel brave, and like a lone explorer. It was cold and windy enough for the Siberian desert, she thought, and there was no one at all in sight. After some hard work, she got down to the smooth sand which had been washed by the last high tide. It was more comfortable because there wasn't so much loose sand to sting all the uncovered bits of her, but everything around her was still violent. The waves hurled themselves at the shore, white clots of foam blew off their peaks and flew wildly up the beach, the sky was racked by the frantic hurrying of torn, ragged clouds.

Priscilla looked back at the sand dunes. There wasn't a sign of anyone from the camp.

'I am alone on an uninhabited island. This is a beach where no human foot but mine has ever trod,' she said.

She looked down at the damp sand. Someone had been

there before her. She saw the tracks of three pairs of human feet, leading away across the beach.

'Bother! So I'm not the first person here,' she thought.

The tracks were odd. Two of them ran evenly, side by side. One was made by bare feet, the other by a pair of shoes with a worn ribbed pattern on the sole. The third track was made by another person wearing ribbed soles, but this person was the odd one, because he walked not forwards, like the other two, but backwards.

'Funny! I wonder why he did that? Could have been some sort of game. Or perhaps he was tracking the other two and wanted to put anyone else who came along off the scent. I'll follow them and see what happens. I might detect a terrible crime, that'd be doing something Cat hasn't,' Priscilla thought.

She started off. Barefoot and Ribby One went steadily on, very near the lashing edge of the waves, but Ribby Two, who walked backwards, was much more erratic. His tracks zigzagged about, sometimes crossing the other tracks, sometimes leaving them and going up the beach for a space, then coming back again. He pressed his toes further in to the sand than his heels, he might be running, whereas Barefoot and Ribby One trod evenly on the whole foot.

'They're talking to each other. Their tracks never cross, but Ribby Two keeps on coming up and going off again. I don't think he was very friendly towards them, if he was there at the same time as they were. Of course it may be that they were tracking him. I wonder why?'

A sudden thought struck Priscilla. The tracks couldn't have been made very long ago. Where had the owners of the feet which had made them got to? She couldn't see a soul on the flat, empty shore. A long, long way ahead a wooden groyne ran down the beach into the sea. Where it met the water, the waves broke into even wilder spray. Priscilla turned back to the tracks. Presently Ribby Two seemed to be becoming friendlier. His footsteps ran more evenly near the other two. He was still walking back-wards.

Priscilla stopped suddenly.

'They stood still here. Barefoot dug the toes of his left foot into the sand, like Tom does when he's arguing. Ribby One walked round him. Or I suppose it could have been Ribby Two. Then one of them scrabbled in the sand. Probably picked up a stone or a shell or something. They must have been here quite a time. There's a lot of shuffling about. Then what happened? If I'm any good at tracking I ought to be able to guess,' Priscilla thought, pleased with herself for what she'd learned so far, and feeling every minute more like Priscilla, and less like that half girl, Puss.

What happened next was extraordinary. Beyond a small patch of seaweed-strewn pebbles, over which the waves were breaking, one track went on alone.

'Where are the others? What happened to the two Ribbys? What did Barefoot do with them?' Priscilla asked .

There was nothing to be seen. There wasn't a single object near by on the flat beach that could possibly have hidden even one body, certainly not two. Except for the far-away groyne, towards which Barefoot's track went steadily on, the beach was empty. The air was full of the tearing, whistling wind, and the sound of the furious water, but the shore was desolate. Priscilla was the only person there.

'Could he have killed them and dragged the bodies off somewhere? But there aren't any marks of things being dragged. And he couldn't have carried two bodies. Perhaps he drowned them, where the pebbly bit was. But two of them! They'd have struggled. There weren't any marks of a struggle,' Priscilla thought.

'Perhaps the tide's gone down since he pushed them in,' Priscilla thought. She felt very clever to have thought of that. But she wasn't sure that the tide was falling. She'd had the impression, as she walked along the beach, that the sea was rising. Each wave seemed to come a little higher up the shore towards her, and the sand above the place where the waves broke was dryer than it would have been with the tide at the ebb.

Like the unknown people who had been there before her, Priscilla stood still.

She could go back. No one had asked her to start on this piece of detection. No one would know, if she just walked back and joined the coach again, that she had given up. She wasn't even sure if she was detecting anything, there might be some ordinary, boring explanation of the three tracks, and the disappearance of two of them, in which case she wouldn't be helping anyone. And it was cold and a bit frightening. And the coach might go off without her. There was every reason to go back.

'I'm cold,' said Priscilla, and she shivered.

'I wish it wasn't just me. If there were more of us I'd go on and find out what's happening, of course I would,' Priscilla said.

A bigger wave than most slapped down not ten yards away and raced up the beach almost to where she stood.

'The tide's coming in. I'm frightened,' Priscilla said.

She looked again at the track that led on towards the distant groyne. The footprints weren't very large, and

somehow this made them the more alarming. ' "Holmes,"
I cried, "A child has done this terrible thing." ' That was
The Sign of Four. Sherlock Holmes and dear stupid Dr
Watson. Priscilla imagined a small man, dark and wiry
and strong, who had somehow disposed of two other
people already, and who now believed he was safe, beyond detection, the other side of that groyne.

'If Cat were here I wouldn't mind so much,' Priscilla
thought.

But Cat wasn't there. Puss was alone.

'I said I'd do something by myself. I'll have to go on.
Perhaps he isn't a murderer, perhaps he's just ordinary.
Perhaps he's tracking, like me,' Priscilla thought.

Barefoot's footprints went straight on, across the beach.
Priscilla followed them. Barefoot walked evenly, he didn't
ever stop, right down on the sand by the sea's edge. Sometimes yards of his track had been washed away by the incoming waves. The tide was certainly rising. And the wind
tore at Priscilla's hair, burned her ears with cold, and
lashed the surface of the sea far out from land into angry
peaks and crevices.

The groyne was a great deal nearer now. Priscilla could
see where the wood was dark with spray. She could see
where some of the beams had rotted and broken. Through
the shouting of the wind and the sea she could hear the
slapping of a bulk of water against the barrier put up by
that battered, shaky wooden groyne. She was near enough
to see that the level of the beach on the further side of the

groyne was lower than on the near side. In a minute or two she'd be able to climb up and to stand on the top horizontal beam, so that she could see where the track continued on the other side.

The wooden tree trunk she walked up was slippery with green slime. Priscilla had to go carefully. She was well up the beach, there was no danger of falling into the sea. She reached the top level and looked across the next reach of sand for more footmarks.

The beach stretched away in front of her, bare. Bare-foot's track stopped here.

Priscilla's heart jumped and pounded, and in spite of the wind she was suddenly hot, then cold with fear. The little man who had got rid of two of his companions must be somewhere very near. He might be hiding below the groyne, waiting to leap out at her. She looked down. A little further down the beach, almost within the reach of the incoming sea, she saw him.

9

That morning Tom had woken up to a scene of terrible destruction. There were splintered spars and damaged paintwork among the boats of the sailing club. There were rents in canvas, one of the hatches had blown open, a storage space was flooded, and one of the half-deckers had been staved in and was only half afloat. It had been a noisy, disturbed night, no one had slept well, everyone was cross.

'No sailing. We'll spend the day tidying and getting everything ship-shape again,' the skipper said.

Tom worked hard. He scrubbed a half-deck, he split his nails untying tight knots in sodden ropes, with four others he pushed a dinghy off a mudbank where the storm had tossed her. He furled canvas and he bailed. He peeled six pounds of potatoes and scraped carrots for a vast stew. Just before lunch he helped to nail down the torn tarpaulin on the roof of the main cabin, and touched up the damaged paint on the side of the houseboat.

'That's the lot. Time off, now, till supper,' Jarvis said after they'd finished the meal.

'Can we take the dinghy up to Poston Broad?'

'No. Wind's getting up again. No sailing today. Go for a walk instead. Or I could take some of you down to the coast if you like.'

'Can we go into Yarmouth? There's a film we might see.'

'If you like. Or I'll take you to the shore. No bathing, but there should be some good waves.'

'I'd rather go to the shore,' Tom said.

Seven of them packed into the van, squashing into the back on top of each other, their mouths pressed against other people's elbows, their backs and behinds pressed by bony knees. Jarvis drove to the nearest bit of coast; a footpath left the road and ran between dykes towards the ramparts of sand dunes which separated the beach from the country inland.

'Who wants to get out here? Tom? Nick? Now let's think about time. I'll be driving back this way about seven o'clock. I'll keep a look-out for you. If you want to walk back it'll take you about an hour and a half to two hours. You mustn't leave it too late, you ought to start somewhere about six-thirty. Has anyone got a watch? The map? Don't do anything silly.' Jarvis drove off.

Tom and Nick followed the footpath. It was cold and windy, and the place was very empty. There wasn't a soul in sight. It wasn't hard going until they reached the foot of the sand dunes and started to climb. And at the top the wind caught them full in the face, a bitter, blustering salt wind straight off the sea. It took Tom by surprise and nearly knocked him over. He crouched in a dip at the top of one of the dunes and looked at the shore below him. It was unlike any beach he'd ever seen. Flat, a mixture of pebbles and sand, pounded by great grey-green waves, it seemed to stretch round the edge of the world, utterly empty, a waste of furious sound and violent action. The only quiet things were the occasional wooden groynes which ran down from the dunes into the angry sea, like lines ruled across pale mottled paper.

'Cold,' said Nick, shivering.

'Let's run.'

'Where to?'

'Down. I want to look at the sea.'

'You're crazy.' But when Tom went, Nick followed.

It was impossible to run. The wind buffeted them with salt spray, pushed them about so that their legs and arms and bodies seemed hardly to belong to them, deafened them. They stumbled on stones. Their eyes and noses streamed, they couldn't see where they were going, they couldn't make each other hear. Tom felt as if his ears would be snatched from off his head by the wet, screaming wind. They fought their way down to the sea's edge and stood just where the foam of the waves glistened and disappeared on the pale stones.

'. . .' Nick said.

'What?'

'. . . going back,' Nick shouted.

'Not yet. Let's go a bit further along.'

He started walking along by the waves, and as before Nick followed. The beach was littered with sea wrack thrown up by the storm. There were mounds of dark seaweed from which fronds, sticking up into the air, waved frantically like the hands of little drowned men. Dead starfish, white cuttlefish bones, fragments of green and red weed torn up by the roots, sodden branches, splinters of spars, empty plastic bottles, lumps of glistening tar were scattered everywhere on the damp stones and sand. There were several huddles of colourless feathers, the remnants of brave birds. Tom thought it looked like a battlefield. It was strewn with the corpses of what had once been living things.

'. . .' Nick said.

'Can't hear!'

'How much further . . . ?'

'I don't know. Let's get to that groyne.'

'What?'

'Said, Let's Get to that Groyne!'

They fought their way along the shore. The groyne was some way off, but Tom was determined to reach it before he turned back. They had all the afternoon and nothing else to do except go back to the houseboat and pack up. Here there was at least a chance that something exciting might happen. There might be a ship in distress; or the storm might throw up some sort of treasure trove. And though the wind was uncomfortable, it was also somehow exciting. It demanded to be fought. It hurled itself against Tom in bursts, it shook him, it worried him as a wild animal worries its prey. Then just as he thought he'd measured its strength, and leaned against it with almost the whole of his weight, it would die down and he'd almost fall. Directly he stood straight again, it came back in its full violence and tried to blow him down.

'WHAT YOU LAUGHING AT?' Nick shouted.

'IT'S FUNNY THE WAY THE WIND BLOWS,' Tom shouted back.

'YOU THINK SO? I THINK IT'S RUDDY AWFUL.'

'WHERE YOU GOING?' Tom asked.

'GOING BACK.'

'WHY? IT'S FUN!'

'I'M FROZEN, THAT'S NOT FUNNY. COME ON!'

Tom shook his head. He wanted to get to the groyne and to climb up to the top, so that he could see the waves from above. It would be like standing on the bows of a ship right out at sea in a storm.

'I'M GOING TO GET TO THE GROYNE,' he said.

'YOU'RE CRAZY!' Nick said again, his breath hot in Tom's ear.

'I'LL CATCH YOU UP,' Tom shouted back. He didn't know if Nick had heard him. He turned back into the wind, and was immediately lost in a world where every-thing was flying around him, a world in which he had no time to think about anything except how to get where he meant to, a world in which he was quite alone. He held his head down and pushed with his shoulders, and leaning against the wind's force as if it had been solid, he went on by himself across the shore.

10

When Priscilla looked down from the top of the groyne about forty minutes later, she saw Tom lying on the sand below her.

'Tom!' she said. She was astonished, relieved, and perhaps somewhere very far inside her, even a little disappointed.

Tom took a long time to open his eyes. He said feebly, 'Oh, it's you.'

'What's the matter? What happened?'

'Fell. Groyne's slippery. Take care.'

'I am taking care. Tom, you'll have to move. The tide's coming up.'

'Can't.'

Priscilla climbed down safely and squatted beside him.

'Where are you hurt?'

'Leg.'

'I can't see anything,' Priscilla said.

Tom said nothing.

'Are you bleeding? I know a lot of first aid now.'

'Don't think so.'

A wave came up and spat half a pint of icy grey water at them, then went away again.

'Tom, you must move up the beach. I'll help.'

'DON'T TOUCH ME!'

'I'm sorry. I'm terribly sorry. But if you stay here you'll be drowned.'

Tom didn't answer.

'TOM! If you don't move up you'll drown. The tide's coming up.'

'Go and fetch someone,' Tom said, not very distinctly.

'All right. Only do try to get a bit further up first.'

'Don't talk. Go!'

Priscilla ran, stumbling, up the beach. The wind was behind her and helped, but it was a slow business. The sand clogged her feet, it was like running in a dream, a nightmare. It was worse on the sand dunes, slipping half a step back for every step on. The harsh stalks of the marram grass hurt her hands when she pulled herself up by them. She was panting and hot and breathless when she reached the top of the dunes, from which she could see the road.

The coach was gone.

Priscilla couldn't believe it. She slithered down into the road and ran along it, back towards the place where the coach had stopped and she and the others had got out. She knew, really, that there wasn't a hope, the road was too straight, there weren't any corners behind which a great fifty-seater coach could be hiding. She had seen at

68

once that there was no coach and no people. They had gone on without her, without noticing that she hadn't come back with Stella and Tina and the others. They'd probably not even bothered to count heads before they set off again, they wouldn't have believed that anyone could want to stay out on the beach in this wind.

She found the place where the coach had stopped. There was a little pool of black oil on the road, tyre marks where it had turned, flattening the grass verge.

She didn't know if there might be any hope of another car coming that way. If there was she could stop it and ask for help. The road looked long and empty, as if nothing had ever driven along it, and nothing ever would. And anyhow she hadn't time to wait and see. All the time she'd been away the tide had been rising. It might have reached Tom by now.

She fought her way up the dunes again, and down on to the beach. The wind seemed stronger and colder than ever, she could hardly stand against it. And she was sure the waves were breaking further up the shore. But Tom was still there, a dark heap, not moving, very near the water's edge. In spite of the wind, Priscilla ran the last fifteen yards.

'Tom! The coach went without me! There wasn't anyone there.'

He looked at her, but didn't speak.

'Tom! I'll have to move you. You're almost in the sea.'

69

Tom still didn't answer.

'I'm going to try to pull you up.'

She put her hands under his shoulders and pulled. Tom cried out with a strange hoarse voice and beat her hands off. She went on pulling. He stopped struggling suddenly, and went limp and very quiet. He was horribly pale. Priscilla thought he had fainted. She wondered if she could move him further from the incoming tide while he was unconscious. Then it wouldn't hurt so much. She tugged, and managed to shift him perhaps two feet up the beach before he began to moan and to push her away again.

'But what am I to do?' Priscilla said to the howling air all round her. She felt desperate. She felt terribly alone. There was nothing that she could do by herself. One person wasn't enough.

'I wish Cat was here,' Puss said.

II

It was Cat who sat limply in the saddle while Lady Evelyn nosed the hedge for edible shoots. It was Cat whose eyes filled with tears of self-pity, and who said to herself. 'But I don't know what to do! I don't know which way to go! I can't get home by myself.' It was Cat who thought of herself out till long after dark in charge of the unpredictable Lady Evelyn, and who panicked.

It was Katherine who blew her nose and began to think.

'It's no good going looking for them. I'd probably just get more lost. Either I'd better stay here and hope they'll come back this way and look for me, or I'd better try to get back to the farm by myself. I wonder if ponies can find their way home like dogs? I expect they can. They're always supposed to go home faster than they go out, so they must know where their homes are.'

She said, 'Home! Home, old lady!' to Lady Evelyn in the kind, governessy sort of voice people use when they make this remark to dogs. Lady Evelyn twitched her intelligent-looking ears and switched her tail – but there were several flies about, and it could have been for them rather than in answer to Katherine – but she didn't make a move in any direction.

'Well, I can't stay here. It might be hours before they come back, and I'm cold. I'll start back the way we came, anyway. That can't be the wrong direction,' Katherine thought, and she kicked Lady Evelyn's sides gently to get her going .

Two hundred yards further on there was a crossroads. No signpost. Katherine couldn't remember having passed it before. She left it to Lady Evelyn to decide which way they should go, and Lady Evelyn, without hesitation, turned left. Katherine felt relieved. Perhaps ponies did have a homing instinct. Perhaps they would get back safely after all.

They had passed several turnings and another cross-roads, before she had her first feeling of unease. It was like going upstairs in the dark and miscounting the treads, so that you expect to take another step up and your foot meets ground on the same level as where you are already standing. It was like going into a room you know by heart, and knowing that something is different, but not being able to tell what. It was like singing a song you have sung a hundred times, but hearing new, strange chords accompanying the melody, so that it becomes one which is foreign to you. It was like being a traveller, and know-ing suddenly, and for no possible apparent reason, that you are going in the wrong direction.

'But I don't know which direction is the right one, so

how can any direction be wrong?' Katherine thought.

She didn't know which direction was which. But she knew with absolute certainty that the road she was on was not the right one.

She turned Lady Evelyn and went back to the cross-roads. Again there was no signpost. Of the four roads which met there, two couldn't be right, the one she had come along, and the second which she had just turned back from. Either of the others might be right, she didn't know which. She turned into the first, and had gone twenty yards along it before the uneasiness grew so strong that she knew she'd have to go back. At the crossroads for the third time, she paused. She felt ordinary again here, any girl on a horse, choosing which way to ride home. In fact there was no choice. She took the last fourth road.

Lady Evelyn trotted gaily, as if she knew this was right. Katherine didn't feel sure of this herself, she only knew that this time it wasn't wrong.

Half a mile further on the road forked. For no reason they took the left hand road. Again it was all right. But a little later, although there hadn't been a crossroads, and they hadn't turned off, Katherine felt the same inward tug, the same unwillingness to go on. She slowed, turned back. When the feeling suddenly lifted, like a fog out of her mind, she saw a turning off, a lane she hadn't noticed. And once in it she knew that it was the way she had to go. It was like a river finding its proper channel below a dam. It was like being a drop of mercury running to join another drop, making a whole as if they'd never been separated. It was like being steel, moving inevitably towards the magnetic north.

'Perhaps I've got the homing instinct,' Katherine thought. Because she certainly wasn't being directed by Lady Evelyn. On more than one occasion Lady Evelyn had been quite definite that she did not want to go where Katherine was determined she should. She'd had to be forced to go in what Katherine knew was the right direction. And this was curious, because the riding school farm was Lady Evelyn's home, and it was not Katherine's.

'I don't feel as if I was going home. It doesn't look like the country round the farm. It's flatter, and it smells different. It doesn't smell of grass and trees and earth. What does it smell like?' Katherine asked.

All sorts of thoughts went through her head. She felt extraordinary. It was extraordinary that she should be here alone, in this strange, flat, windy country, riding a horse she wasn't used to, not knowing where she was, choosing her direction by a feeling she didn't understand, without an idea of where the place might be she was aiming at. It was like being another person. She had been frightened, and she still was, but in a way it was because she was frightened that she had to go on. It was like being on the other side of fear. She hadn't forgotten her terror that Lady Evelyn would bolt, or that she might still be wandering in these little roads when night fell, but beyond these fears there was a need to go on, to get somewhere. She had to obey this need although she didn't understand it. And it seemed to grow as the smell brought by the wind, and the wind itself, grew stronger. It reminded her of something and she couldn't think what. Something good, something she'd like to remember. Happiness, the rest of the family, a holiday, laughing, feeling pleased and clever and terribly alive. Her father saying, 'You wouldn't call the Queen your cousin,' meaning that they were on top of the world, that day, the Queen couldn't have had more. They? She knew. It had been when they'd all been out in the boat from Newlyn, mackerel fishing, and she and Puss had been the only ones whose line had caught a fish. A triumphant, splendid, victorious day.

And the smell was the smell of the sea.

The wind, howling round her now, uncomfortably strong, was a sea wind. It smelled of salt, and seaweed. It was damp and fresh and good.

She was riding towards the shore, and she was going there because Puss was calling for her. She knew it as certainly as if she'd heard Puss's voice in her ears.

She remembered that the sand and the sea excited ponies and made them wild and difficult to control. But she went on. She knew now what she had to do. At each meeting of the roads she slowed, and tried the different paths. When one turned out wrong she knew she had to go back and try again. When she was right, she knew because she could feel the rightness deep inside her. And all the time

the air grew colder and more salty, and the wind blew stronger, in gusts that seemed as if they might blow her out of the saddle. Lady Evelyn snorted and danced. In the distance Katherine could hear the roar of waves breaking, beating and sucking at a pebbly, sandy shore.

They came out at last on to a long road, running straight across the country from nowhere to nowhere. On the opposite side of it was a line of sand dunes. The grass on them was flattened and stretching in the sea wind.

Katherine rode Lady Evelyn up the dunes. They had to go sideways, and they slipped and scrambled on the loose footing, and in the pits and rabbit holes. The wind hit them hard as they reached the top, blinding Katherine and buffeting the mare so that she staggered. Through the sand and her streaming hair, and the water in her eyes, Katherine tried to search the beach, but she could see nothing. She knew, though, that she had to go down towards the sea, and she urged Lady Evelyn over the soft sand, into the fury of the wind. She'd never thought she'd be able to make the pony do anything it was determined not to do, but this time her determination to get where she had to was even stronger. They pushed their way towards the sea, towards the only landmark on that waste of battering wind and hurling water : a wooden groyne. Katherine could see now that under the groyne, very near the water's edge, there were two figures. Long before she was near enough to recognize them, Katherine knew who they were and why she'd come.

She slipped off Lady Evelyn's back and led her, it was quicker, down to where the groyne ran into the boiling, turbulent sea.

'I thought you were never coming. Help me move Tom up before the tide gets any higher,' Puss said the moment Cat reached her.

'I'll just tie Lady Evelyn up first. You did want me to come, didn't you?' Cat asked.

'Of course. I was *willing* you, silly. Buck up, or we're all going to get drowned here together.'

12

The holiday ended with trouble for everyone. Tom escaped most of it by being in hospital with a leg in plaster. He missed Jarvis's remarks about boys who were old enough to be responsible for getting back to base on time, or who should be able to climb over a slippery log without falling like babies. Tom lay in bed and thought that perhaps girls weren't so feeble after all. Cat had ridden off, she'd *galloped* up the beach, to fetch help. Puss had stayed by him for what had felt like hours. Even when the waves had come right up and almost broken over them, she hadn't moved so that she was safe and dry, she'd tugged him inch by inch a little further up the beach, though he'd yelled at her to leave him alone, tried to hit her to make her stop hurting him. Afterwards, in the ambulance, he'd said, 'Sorry, Puss,' and she hadn't corrected him and said, 'I'm *Priscilla*,' she'd just said, 'It's all right. Sorry I had to hurt you.'

Priscilla found herself in disgrace. After its brief stop near the sea, the coach had gone on without anyone noticing that one girl was missing, and Laurie, the camp leader, was annoyed with herself for this mistake, and twice as angry with Priscilla for being the cause of it. The coach had made a second, longer stop in Yarmouth half an hour later, and it was when the party collected again after tea in a cockle bar, and a round of fruit machines in an amusement arcade, that heads were counted and it was found that one was missing. Laurie had spent over an hour searching for Priscilla all over Yarmouth, and had come away leaving messages with the police and the proprietors of every place they'd visited. When Priscilla finally arrived at the camp at half past ten that night, in an ambulance – it was the quickest way of getting her from the hospital where she'd left Tom, back to the camp site – no one seemed pleased to see her. Laurie was furious. Stella and Alison were angry at being woken up when she crawled into the tent they shared with her. It didn't help that Priscilla pointed out to Laurie that anyone could have seen her leave the coach, and that no one had told her when to come back. 'Stella must have noticed I wasn't there, she was sitting next to me,' she said.

'Don't try to put the blame on Stella. You shouldn't have gone off by yourself like that,' Laurie said, frightened and angry.

'I thought we'd stopped so we could go on to the beach.'

'Didn't it occur to you to look round and see if any of the others were with you?'

'You're always telling us to be independent, not to do

everything in crowds. Anyway, you could have shouted at me to say I was to come back.'

'No one could have shouted against that wind.'

'You didn't try. You didn't bother to see if we were all there. It wasn't my fault. It was yours.'

'Go to bed!' Laurie shouted. And Priscilla went. She said to Stella, who woke up, grumbling, 'Why didn't you tell Laurie I hadn't come back from the beach?'

'It wasn't my business where you were.'

'Didn't you see I wasn't anywhere on the coach?'

'I didn't look.'

'But you can't just not have noticed ... !'

'Stop talking. I want to go to sleep.'

'I don't care. I found Tom. I saved him from being drowned. I bet Stella wouldn't have gone on tracking all by herself, she'd have been much too frightened.' Priscilla thought, huddled in her sleeping-bag, trying to get warm by curling herself up into as small a parcel as possible. Later, just before she fell asleep, she thought, 'It was a good thing Cat came. I suppose she saved Tom too.'

Katherine came off worst of all. She'd had to ride Lady Evelyn back to the farm after dark, guided by a young policeman on a bicycle. He saw her into the farmhouse, then rode away, leaving Katherine to explain what had happened and why she was so late. But Diana was too angry to listen to any explanations. She wasn't concerned with what Katherine had been doing, or what had happened to anyone else, she couldn't think about anything except the pony.

'What do you think you're doing, keeping Lady Evelyn out till this hour? She's dead beat. She won't be fit to go out for a week.'

'I didn't mean to. I got lost . . .'

'Lost? We were all together, weren't we, till you went off on your own?'

'I didn't. I did get lost, truly, Diana . . .'

'You couldn't get lost round here. You must have been able to see where the rest of us were.'

'I didn't *want* to be left all alone!' Katherine cried out.

'If you got lost, then, how did you find your way back?'

'The hospital telephoned the police station . . .'

'The *hospital*?'

'Puss went there in the ambulance with Tom, and told them about me. I couldn't go with them because of Lady Evelyn.'

'I don't understand a word you're saying,' Diana said.

'You don't listen!' Katherine said. She couldn't believe, the next moment, that she'd really spoken to Diana like that.

'Go on, then.'

'And they sent a policeman on a bicycle, with a lamp, to meet me, and he showed me how to get back here.'

'Do you realize you've had that pony out on the roads for *eight* hours?'

84

'I'm sorry. I said, I didn't mean to.'

'I suppose you wouldn't care if she was lamed for life?'

'You talk as if I'd wanted it to happen. And I'm tired too, I'm dead,' Katherine said.

'You can't go to bed till you've unsaddled Lady Evelyn and seen to her. You know the rules,' Diana said.

Lady Evelyn didn't seem much the worse for her adventure. She was tired, but not too tired to eat. When Katherine gave her the mash which was her evening meal, she nuzzled Katherine's shoulder before dropping her long nose into the pail of food. She smelled deliciously of horse, her warm skin was satiny. Katherine looked round the stables, and saw that she was the only human there. She put her arms round Lady Evelyn's long sinewy neck, and her cheek on the brown silk skin. She suddenly loved Lady Evelyn. She wasn't frightened of her any more. In spite of Diana she went to bed almost happy.

After the holidays, the school term. Tom went back, glorious, in a plaster cast. His friends wrote their names and rude messages on it, the wittier ones wrote limericks. It got dirtier and dirtier, and at last he shed it like a snake its skin. But he had kept it for weeks, and remained all that time a hero. He told his story very fairly. He had gone exploring by himself on the North Sea coast, had fallen and broken his leg. The tide was rising, he couldn't have moved without help, he'd certainly have drowned if his sisters hadn't arrived in the nick of time and saved him. It was the most dramatic adventure that anyone at his

school had had that year. Tom wrote a first class composition on *The Most Extraordinary Day of My Life* for his half-term holiday task, and won the school essay prize. The composition was read aloud to the form, and now everyone had heard the story.

'Why weren't you all having holidays together, you and your sisters?' Dickinson asked him.

'We went on separate sorts of holidays. Neither of them came sailing. One was camping, the other was at a riding school.'

'Which of them found you on the beach?'

'The camping one. She'd followed my tracks across the beach – thought she'd uncovered a crime, and then it was only me,' said Tom.

'How did the other one know where you were? Did she follow your tracks too?'

'No. She just sort of thought of looking for us there,' Tom said.

'Isn't that rather fantastic? How could she?' Dickinson asked.

'They're twins, my sisters.'

'Do they always do everything the same? At the same time? Are they exactly alike?' Dickinson asked.

'No. They're different kinds of people, really, only they sort of belong.'

'Reciprocal?' asked Dickinson, who had a scientific background.

'What's that?' asked Tom, who hadn't.

'Dickinson says you're reciprocal,' Tom said to Puss and Cat later.

'What's that mean?'

'Means you're separate, like two bits of a machine, but you need each other to work properly. If Puss hadn't found me, Cat wouldn't have come to help her. If Cat hadn't come, Puss wouldn't have saved me from drowning.'

'You sound as if all we had to do was to look after you,' Puss remarked.

'It might work for other things as well, I suppose.'

'If we'd always done everything the same you'd probably be drowned by now,' Puss said.

'All right! I wasn't getting at you. I was just saying, you can be separate.'

'We are separate.'

'We're two different people.'

'I'm Priscilla and she's Katherine.'

'We're not just PussCat any more.'

'I said, all *right*! Don't bite me! I only said you did all right when you did things together. What's wrong with that?'

'Nothing,' said Puss.

'That's fine,' said Cat.

About the Author

Catherine Storr was born in London and has lived there for most of her life. She was educated at St Paul's Girls' School and at Newnham College, Cambridge. During the last war she married and had three daughters, for whom many of her first children's books were written. She qualified as a doctor and practised medicine for fourteen years but has now given it up in order to have more time for writing. Now that her daughters have grown up she writes also for adults, but thinks that she will probably always want to write for children too because they share her enjoyment of a story and understand that fantasy and reality are not opposing but different ways of looking at the same thing. Also in Puffins: *Clever Polly and the Stupid Wolf*, *Polly and the Wolf Again*, and *Marianne Dreams*.

Some Other Young Puffins

Bandicoot and his Friends

Violet Philpott

Lion promised his friends a surprise when he came home from India, but no one expected anything half as nice as friendly, funny, furry little Bandicoot, who was so kind and clever when any of his friends were in trouble.

Adventures of Sam Pig

Alison Uttley

Ten funny and magical stories about Alison Uttley's best-loved creation. For children of five to nine.

Hallo, Aurora!

Anne-Cath. Vestly

At first Aurora didn't like the new flat much, with no friends and a frightening thing called a lift to deal with, but it was fun helping Father at the supermarket and the launderette, or with Socrates at the baby clinic, and even better when Knut helped make the Christmas biscuits.

Little Bear's Feather *and* Run for Home

Evelyn Davies

Two separate stories on similar themes: Little Bear is a Red Indian Chief's son, Matthew the child of English settlers in Red Indian territory. They both have a dream and both find they must be brave in an unexpected way to realize it.

The Sawdust Secret

Jean Willis

How Sandy, John and Mike investigate the disappearance of some valuable antiques.

Mrs Pinny and the Blowing Day

Helen Morgan

Washday – and a windy magic blows over Mrs Pinny, her washing, and even the local train service.

The Adventures of Mandy Duck

Donald Bisset

A remarkable day in the life of an adventurous duck provides the framework for a witty set of stories within a story.

Joseph's Bear

Evelyn Davies

The bear was the very best thing that Joseph had ever owned, but when you love something you may have to make a hard decision.

Stories for Five-Year-Olds
Stories for Six-Year-Olds
Stories for Seven-Year-Olds
Stories for Eight-Year-Olds

edited by Sara and Stephen Corrin

Celebrated anthologies of stories especially selected for each age group and tested in the classroom by the editors.

Where Matthew Lives

Teresa Verschoyle

Happy stories about a little boy exploring his new home, a cottage tucked away by the sea.

Tales of Joe and Timothy
Joe and Timothy Together

Dorothy Edwards

Friendly, interesting stories about two small boys living in different flats in a tall, tall house, and the good times they have together.

Umbrella Thursday *and* A Helping Hand

Janet McNeill

Good deeds sometimes have funny results, as the two little girls in these stories discover.

Candy Floss *and* Impunity Jane

Rumer Godden

Two stories about dolls by an author who understands their feelings.

A Gift from Winklesea

Helen Cresswell

Dan and Mary buy a beautiful stone like an egg as a present for their mother – and then it hatches out, into the oddest animal they ever saw.

HEARD ABOUT THE PUFFIN CLUB?

... it's a way of finding out more about Puffin books and
authors, of winning prizes (in competitions), sharing jokes,
a secret code, and perhaps seeing your name in print!
When you join you get a copy of our magazine, *Puffin Post*,
sent to you four times a year, a badge and a membership
book.

For details of subscription and an application form, send
a stamped addressed envelope to:

The Puffin Club Dept A
Penguin Books Limited
Bath Road
Harmondsworth
Middlesex UB7 ODA

and if you live in Australia, please write to:

The Australian Puffin Club
Penguin Books Australia Limited
P.O. Box 257
Ringwood
Victoria 3134